DEC 2 2 2020

DISCARDED OR WITHDRAWN
GREAT NECK LIBRARY

BRIGHT IDEA BOOKS

AIR FORCE ONE

Protecting the President's Plane

by Kaitlyn Duling

CAPSTONE PRESS
a capstone imprint

Bright Ideas is published by Capstone Press, an imprint of Capstone.
1710 Roe Crest Drive
North Mankato, Minnesota 56003
www.capstonepub.com

Copyright © 2020 by Capstone. All rights reserved. No part of this publication may be reproduced in whole or in part, or stored in a retrieval system, or transmitted in any form or by any means, electronic, mechanical, photocopying, recording, or otherwise, without written permission of the publisher.

Library of Congress Cataloging-in-Publication Data
ISBN: 978-1-5435-9056-2 (library hardcover)
ISBN: 978-1-5435-9057-9 (eBook PDF)

Summary: Describes how Air Force One keeps the U.S. president safe while flying, including descriptions of the plane's security features.

Image Credits
Alamy: Niday Picture Library, 14–15; AP Images: Pablo Martinez Monsivais, 23; iStockphoto: BrianEKushner, cover, DaveAlan, 17, Deepak Sethi, 30–31, jdwfoto, 6–7, mvp64, 8–9, 28; Newscom: Cecil Stoughton/UPI/John F. Kennedy Presidential Library & Museum, 13, Paul Morse/White House/CNP, 18; Shutterstock Images: 1000 Words, 10–11, Christopher Halloran, 5, Davide Calabresi, 26–27, Gerckens-Photo-Hamburg, 25, Guy RD, 20–21
Design Elements: Shutterstock Images

Editorial Credits
Editor: Charly Haley; Designer: Laura Graphenteen; Production Specialist: Dan Peluso

All internet sites appearing in back matter were available and accurate when this book was sent to press.

Printed in the United States of America.
PA99

TABLE OF CONTENTS

CHAPTER ONE
WHAT IS AIR FORCE ONE?.. 4

CHAPTER TWO
PRESIDENTS ON AIR FORCE ONE 12

CHAPTER THREE
SAFETY FEATURES 16

CHAPTER FOUR
LEADING WHILE FLYING 22

CHAPTER FIVE
A NEW AIR FORCE ONE 24

Glossary 28
Trivia 29
Activity 30
Further Resources 32
Index 32

CHAPTER 1

WHAT IS Air Force One?

The president of the United States needs to fly somewhere far away. The president's airplane is different from most. The plane is Air Force One. It is very safe.

Barack Obama flew on Air Force One many times as president.

Why does Air Force One need to be safe? It carries the leader of the United States. It carries the president's team too. **Secret Service** officers are always inside. They guard the president. The president's team and family sit up front. **Reporters** sit in the back.

The Secret Service keeps the president safe all the time. This includes when the president is traveling.

OTHER PLANES

Sometimes other planes fly with Air Force One. They carry Secret Service officers. They give the president more protection.

Air Force One is a huge jet. It is white and blue with a gold stripe. The American flag is painted on its tail. The presidential **seal** is on its side. Anyone who sees the plane knows the president flies in it.

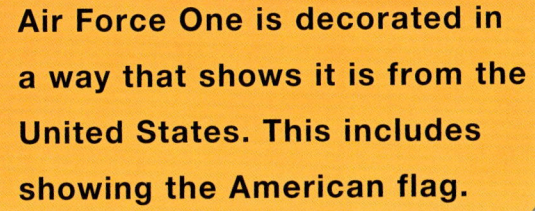

Air Force One is decorated in a way that shows it is from the United States. This includes showing the American flag.

AIR FORCE TWO

Sometimes the vice president uses the president's plane. Then it is called Air Force Two.

TWO PLANES

There are two Air Force One planes. They look the same. While one gets fixed, the other flies. The planes fly all over the world.

A bulletproof car usually waits for the president once Air Force One has landed.

Air Force One takes the president to meetings. It takes the president on fun trips too. It is comfortable inside. It has a gym and kitchen.

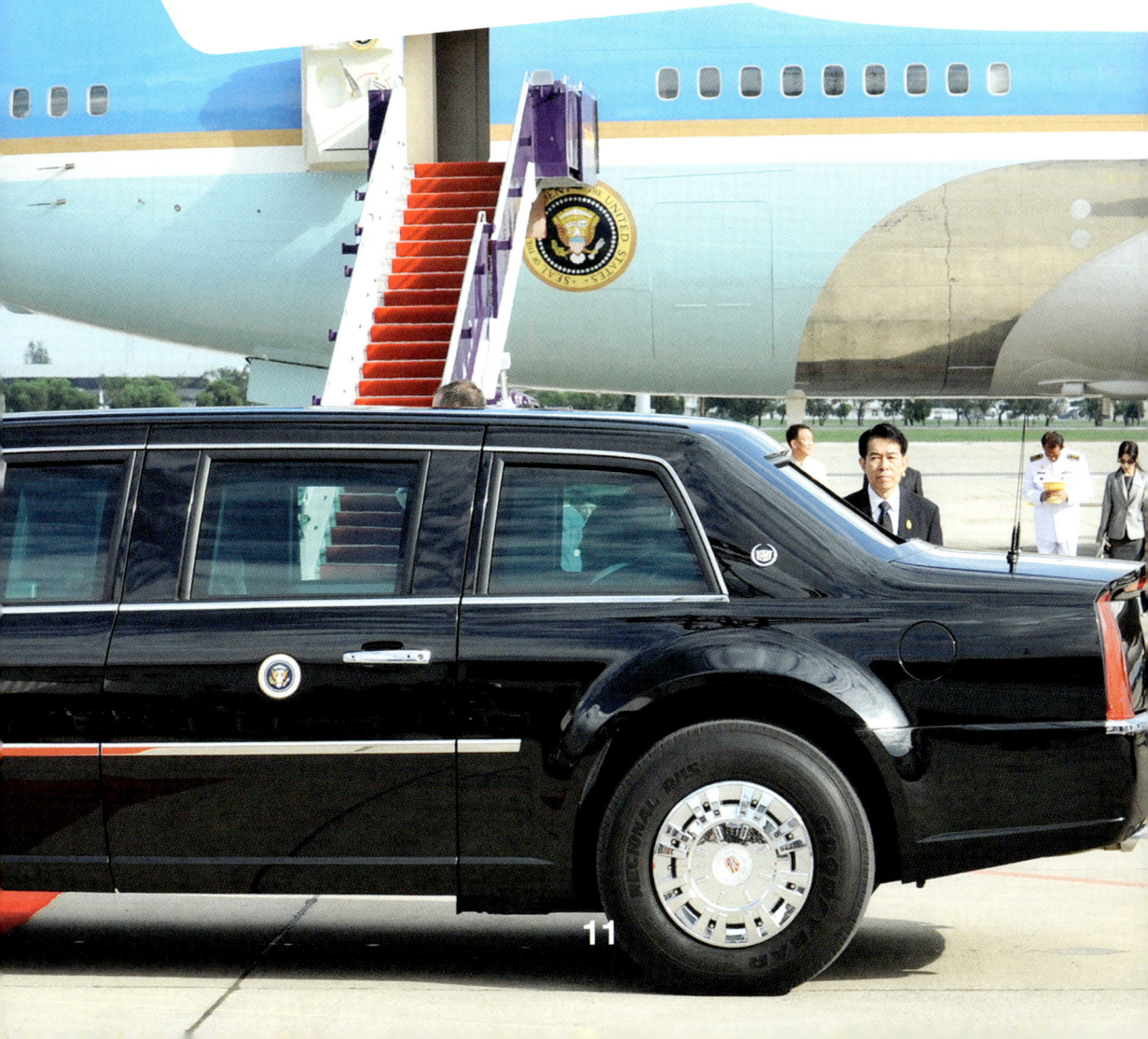

CHAPTER 2

PRESIDENTS ON Air Force One

Presidents used to ride in trains. Some rode in cars. They did not fly until 1943. The first Air Force One flew in 1962. President John F. Kennedy used the plane.

THE SACRED COW

Franklin D. Roosevelt was the first U.S. president to fly in an airplane. His plane was called the Sacred Cow.

The Air Force One plane that carried President John F. Kennedy (right) and his wife, Jacqueline, was called SAM 26000.

Sometimes Air Force One is involved with sad events. President Kennedy was killed in Texas in 1963. Air Force One brought his body to Washington, D.C.

President George W. Bush flew on the plane on September 11, 2001. There was an attack against the United States that day. Bush was visiting a school in Florida when it happened. Officers thought the president might be attacked. He went on Air Force One to be safe. Then he flew to Washington, D.C.

Lyndon B. Johnson (middle) was sworn in as president on Air Force One after President Kennedy died.

CHAPTER 3

SAFETY Features

Air Force One has many safety features. Most of them are secret. Only a few people know everything about the plane.

The plane has thick windows. Bullets cannot go through them. The plane can also release **flares**. These show bright lights. They are hot. They confuse enemy weapons that follow heat.

Some of the plane's safety features are hidden within its body.

President George W. Bush used the phone while traveling on Air Force One to talk with leaders of other countries.

Air Force One has a special skin. It covers the plane. This skin protects against certain attacks.

Air Force One protects the president's work too. The plane has 85 phones. Some are for secret information. Messages on those phones are sent in **code**.

FLYING AND LANDING

Air Force One can fly thousands of miles in one trip. It does not stop for fuel during a trip. It **refuels** while flying.

When it does stop, Air Force One lands on an empty runway. A team helps the president rush to a car. Sometimes the president gets on a helicopter instead. The team makes sure the president is safe.

The president has a group of helicopters too. Each helicopter is called Marine One.

CHAPTER 4

LEADING WHILE Flying

Air Force One has everything the president might need. There is always a doctor on board. **Crew** members work inside. There are places to sleep. There are TVs.

The president must always be able to lead, even while flying. Air Force One has an office. The president can use the internet on the plane.

President Donald Trump (left) in the Air Force One office in 2017

CHAPTER 5

A NEW Air Force One

The government is working on a new Air Force One. It may be ready by 2024. Two planes will be made.

The new planes will fly farther without refueling than the old ones. They will fly faster too.

The new Air Force One planes will be Boeing 747s like the old ones.

The new Air Force One will be longer. It will be wider and heavier. It might be a different color. It will cost billions of dollars.

The new planes will have better safety features. The military is keeping them secret. But people know the new Air Force One will protect the president.

Air Force One may look different in the future. But it will always keep the president safe.

GLOSSARY

code
a set of symbols, letters, or numbers that can be used to reveal a hidden message

crew
a group of people who work together

flare
an object that gives off a short burst of hot light

refuel
to get more fuel

reporter
a person who creates news stories for newspapers, websites, TV, or radio

seal
a symbol that shows a certain thing, such as a symbol for the office of the U.S. president

Secret Service
a group of officers who protect the president

TRIVIA

1. Air Force One has three floors inside.

2. Each Air Force One aircraft is fitted with four jet engines that propel the plane to a top speed of 630 miles (1,010 kilometers) per hour.

3. When it's not in use, Air Force One is stored at Joint Base Andrews, a military base in Maryland.

4. The phones on Air Force One are color coded. White phones are for everyday calls. Beige phones are secure lines meant for sharing important information and secrets.

ACTIVITY

MAKE YOUR OWN AIRPLANE

Airplane designs have improved over the years. Planes fly faster and farther than ever before. Each new version of Air Force One is a little bigger, heavier, and more secure. With a little practice, you can design a great airplane too.

You can fold a simple airplane out of a piece of paper. Create your own design. If you need help, ask a parent or friend. You can also go online or to the library to find instructions for folding paper airplanes.

When your plane is ready, toss it into the air and watch it fly! Once your plane lands on the ground, you can use a ruler or measuring tape to see how far it flew. Then see what happens when you change your design. Does it fly farther? Faster? Does it turn or fly straight? Record what you see and try to improve your design.

FURTHER RESOURCES

Interested in learning more about protecting the president? Check out these resources:

Nagelhout, Ryan. *Air Force One*. New York: Gareth Stevens Publishing, 2015.

Shea, Therese. *A Career as a Secret Service Agent*. New York: PowerKids Press, 2016.

U.S. Secret Service Website
www.secretservice.gov

Want to learn more about airplanes? Check out these resources:

DK Find Out! History of Aircraft
www.dkfindout.com/uk/transport/history-aircraft

Prior, Jennifer. *Take Off! All About Airplanes*. Huntington Beach, Calif.: Teacher Created Materials, 2011.

Air Force Two, 9

Bush, George W., 14

flares, 17
fuel, 20, 25

helicopters, 20

Kennedy, John F., 12, 14

reporters, 6
Roosevelt, Franklin D., 13

Secret Service, 6, 7

Washington, D.C., 14